SARAH, ALSO KNOWN AS HANNAH

Lillian Hammer Ross
illustrations by Helen Cogancherry

Albert Whitman & Company • Morton Grove • Illinois

Dedicated to my mother,
Frieda Kamornick Hammer, for it is her story.

Library of Congress Cataloging-in-Publication Data

Ross, Lillian Hammer.
    Sarah, also known as Hannah / Lillian Hammer Ross ;
illustrated by Helen Cogancherry.

    p.   cm.

    Summary: When twelve-year-old Sarah leaves the
Ukraine for America in her sister's place, she must use
her sister's passport and her sister's name, Hannah.
ISBN 0-8075-7237-3
    [1. Emigration and immigration—Fiction.]
I. Cogancherry, Helen, ill. II. Title.
PZ7.R7196965Sar   1994
[Fic]—dc20   93-29601
                                                        CIP
                                                        AC

Design by Lucy Smith.

Text copyright © 1994 by Lillian Hammer Ross.
Illustrations copyright © 1994 by Helen Cogancherry.
Published in 1994 by Albert Whitman & Company,
6340 Oakton Street, Morton Grove, Illinois 60053-2723.
Published simultaneously in Canada
by General Publishing, Limited, Toronto.
Printed in the United States of America.
10 9 8 7 6 5 4 3 2

The lines of poetry on page 63 are excerpted from Emma
Lazarus's poem, "The New Colossus," written in 1883.

The writing of this book began when I asked my mother to tell me how she came to America. She was ninety-one years old, and, as with many older people, her remembrances of a past life were keener than her memory of current events.

"Perhaps what you tell me will become a book," I said, smiling.

My mother shook her head. "A very sad story. My mother sent me away. She sent me away to America." There were tears in her eyes.

"Oh, Mom." I took her hand. "If you had stayed in Lisec, you would never have met Dad, and I would never have been born."

She nodded and looked into my eyes. "And you could never write my story."

My dear mother died, in her sleep, at the age of ninety-four.

L.H.R.
October, 1993

GREAT
BRITAI

TO NEW YORK

PORTUGAL

SPAIN

SARAH,

We sat shiva. My family and I sat in our house during the seven days following my father's death. We then observed the customary thirty days of mourning. My father, whose prayers we had heard morning, noon, and night, was gone. My father, whose strong arms had comforted me, was gone. My father, my storyteller, was gone.

Women of the village told us we had to get on with our lives. One day, with tears streaming down her face, Mama wrote a letter to America.

> *To my dear brother Benjamin,*
> *My husband, Joseph, has died, leaving me with two grown daughters and two small sons. The girls are of marriageable age, twelve and sixteen years. I have no means to provide them with a dowry, and I fear they will remain unmarried. Life is easier where you live than here in Lisec. Could you send for both girls? I will be able to manage with Avram and Chaim. I still have our home; I took in boarders*

before my husband died, so there is some money. I
am worried about my daughters' future lives.
Please, Benjamin, let me know if you are willing
to take Hannah and Sarah.

    Greetings to Fayge.

      Your sister Leitcha.

When the postman arrived in his horse-drawn wagon, Mama gave him the letter. Then, for months, when we heard someone call, "Postman!" we ran to the square in front of the school. We waited while he called the names of lucky ones who had received letters. Finally, one day, the postman shouted, "Leitcha, a letter from America!"

Hannah, Avram, Chaim, and I clustered around Mama. As we walked home, she read:

My dear sister Leitcha,

    News of your husband's death saddened me and
my wife. We would like to help. We can afford to
buy passage for only one child. Hannah, the older, is
my choice. As a sixteen-year-old girl, it will be
easier for her to find work in a factory. Later, if she
saves her money, both she and I will send for you and
the other children. Hannah's tickets for the train
and ship will arrive in the next mail. The man for
whom I work has loaned me extra money. This has
enabled me to purchase Hannah a third-class ticket

so she will not have to travel by steerage class. She must go to Stanislav for her passport. God willing, Fayge and I will see our niece soon.

   Your brother Benjamin

p.s. I am sending a picture of Fayge and me. Hannah will need to recognize us when we meet her on Ellis Island.

In bed that night, Hannah and I hugged each other and cried. We were sisters, and we were friends. Except for size, we looked enough alike to be twins. "Like two peas in a pod," Papa had always said. Now, Uncle Benjamin's letter brought news that we would be separated. It was as though this unknown uncle had come between us. But Hannah reassured me she would work hard in America, would save her money, and would send for me.

We whispered in the dark about America and what Hannah would find. Were the streets really paved with gold? Were there Indians who scalped people? And what of men who kidnapped young girls and forced them into slavery? We shared feelings of joy and fear.

"Tomorrow you must go to Stanislav to get a passport," Mama told Hannah while we ate breakfast.

"Me too!" Avram and Chaim banged their spoons on the table. "Me too!"

"When you are older." Mama smiled at the boys. "Sarah, you will go with Hannah."

"May we visit with Mima Civia?" I loved Mama's cousin. She was as round as a dumpling, and at her house, we could do whatever we wanted.

"Another time." Mama sighed and shook her head. "I want you to come straight home."

Hannah reached for Mama's hand. "Papa would have been happy I was going to America."

I looked down at my shoes so no one would see my face. I felt angry and jealous. Angry at Uncle Benjamin and jealous because I wanted to go to America with Hannah.

The next day, Hannah and I rode in our neighbor Yossel's wagon to Stanislav to order Hannah's passport. Stanislav was a big city. So many people, so many buildings, so many horses with beautiful carriages! Everyone seemed to be in a hurry.

Yossel took us to the building for passports. He said he had taken many villagers to Stanislav for just this purpose. "Wait for me at the photographer's, and I will take you home."

The building for passports was tall and made of brick. It had a tower with a big clock that bonged every fifteen minutes and bonged to count out the hour. I jumped with the first bong. Nothing in Lisec had a sound like that!

Hannah answered all the questions the man at the desk asked, and she showed him her birth certificate. He told us where to have her passport picture taken.

It was strange to walk on a boardwalk and hear the click of our heels on the wood. At home, we walked in the dirt, and our footsteps were silent.

The photographer's shop was dark and smelled musty. Hannah and I held hands. Hannah told the man she needed a picture for her passport. He smiled and wished her good luck. He told her to stand in front of a huge painting of a cloudless sky.

The photographer's camera looked like a black box. It stood on three tall legs and was covered with a mysterious black cloth. The photographer put his head under the cloth and told Hannah not to move.

Then out he came. He helped a boy pour white powder on a tray fastened to the end of a tall stick. The boy lifted the stick and the tray over his head. The man struck a match and set fire to a string that dangled from the end of the tray.

Hannah looked scared. I held my breath, afraid she would be set on fire.

The photographer put his head under the black cloth

again. "Don't move!" he called. The boy's tray exploded, Hannah and I jumped, then giggled in embarrassment.

"Your passport with your picture should arrive at your house in three weeks."

Hannah told the man where we lived and gave him a half krone, the cost of the picture.

We walked out into the bright light of Stanislav and looked for Yossel.

Every day Hannah, Avram, Chaim, and I ran to the village square in front of the school, to wait for the postman. "Run! Run!" the boys shouted as they raced ahead, then turned to run back to us.

"I'll miss all of you," Hannah said every day, and sometimes she cried.

"And I'll miss you. I'll be the only big sister."

"I'll save my money, Sarah, and no matter how long it takes, I'll send for you. It might take two or three years, but I'll save every penny I earn." She reached for my hand. "Cheer up. In three years, you'll be fifteen. That's still one year younger than I am right now."

Three weeks later, when the postman stopped in the square, he called Hannah's name and handed her two envelopes. One had her passport from Stanislav. The second envelope held a letter from Uncle Benjamin and Hannah's tickets to America.

Laughing, Hannah jumped up and down, her face flushed. The boys and I jumped with her.

As we ran home, Hannah waved her tickets to our neighbors. "I'm going to America!" she shouted.

We burst into the house and danced around Mama. "To America! Hannah's going to America!"

Mama didn't look happy. She wore the same face as when we had sat shiva. "Quiet," she whispered. "Shah, shah."

We stopped dancing.

"Sit down." Mama sat facing us in her rocking chair. It was as though life had stopped. All the world kept twirling while the four of us froze.

"What I have to say is very sad," Mama said.

I held my breath. Was Mama sick like Papa had been?

"I have given this great thought. And I have prayed for guidance." She reached out and touched Hannah's shoulder. "I agreed to send you to America, Hannah, but now I have second thoughts."

"What do you mean, second thoughts?" gasped Hannah.

Mama sat in silence. The quiet pressed against me. Then she spoke. "We all miss Papa. Life is not easy without a man." Mama looked at Hannah. "It's true, we have boarders in the house to help with money, but . . ."

Hannah was breathing hard. Avram and Chaim looked scared.

"Hannah," Mama said, "if you go to America, I will be left with Sarah and the boys." It seemed difficult for her to speak. "You are sixteen years old. You know how to use my sewing machine, and you have already earned money sewing for our neighbors."

Hannah moved closer to me. I put my arm around her. Avram put his arm around Chaim.

"Whatever money you've earned, Hannah, has helped toward our living, and you have put aside a little for your dowry." Mama looked at me. My stomach jumped. "I think it would be better if Sarah went to America."

"Mama! You can't do this to me!" screamed Hannah. "Please, Mama, I beg of you. This is my golden opportunity." Tears rolled down her cheeks. "What are you doing to me?"

Hannah knelt by Mama, put her head on Mama's lap, and sobbed, "Mama, oh, Mama. You are taking my life away from me!"

I felt like a stone. Hannah looked like she was being tortured. The stone broke, and I burst into tears.

Fear grabbed me. Mama wanted to send me away. I wasn't any help to her. "I'm only twelve years old. I don't want to go to America all by myself." I choked on my sobs.

"Hannah wants to go to America, Mama. Let Hannah go. Please, let Hannah go."

"No," Mama said in a voice that didn't sound like Mama. "It's better if you go, Sarah. You will find work. You will send half your money home, and you will save half your money." Mama looked at Hannah's grief-stricken face. "Later, Uncle Benjamin and Sarah will buy tickets for all of us."

Hannah sat up straight. "It's unfair, Mama. I'm older. I'm the one who should go to America. I have my passport. I have my tickets."

I joined Hannah. "It *is* unfair. I'm scared to go alone. I've only been to Stanislav." I waved my hands as if to brush away a bad dream. "Oh, Mama, please. I don't want to go to America by myself."

Mama stood. "It's decided. You will use Hannah's passport, and you will go to America. No more talk." She left the room.

I looked at Hannah's tear-stained face. I felt Mama had given me Hannah's life. My life in America would not only be my life, it would be Hannah's life as well. I put my arms around her waist, and we stood as one.

The following weeks were like living in a fairy tale in which tasks had to be completed so the princess might be saved. But no one was being saved. Hannah felt she was lost and I was saved. I felt we both were lost.

A strange, unpleasant feeling drifted through the house. Words were few. Even Avram and Chaim stayed away from us. Mama avoided us, working in the kitchen and seeing to the needs of the boarders. I felt she cared for them more than she cared for Hannah and me. And why not? They paid her for their room and their food. I couldn't give Mama even one pfennig.

Why didn't Mama talk to us? Was she silent because of her disappointment in sending only one child to America? Did she act like this because she missed Papa? Was she just as unhappy as we were?

Hannah and I sewed me a dress and a coat from material Mama had bought. We even worked on a bag made of leftover coat material. Our anger and sadness were spoken in whispers.

Mama sent me to the shoemaker, who traced a line around my feet while I stood on an old newspaper. I was to have new shoes that laced to the middle of my leg. It was strange to be so unhappy while at the same time so excited to have a pair of new shoes.

This was the first time I had my own new clothes. I had always worn Hannah's outgrown things. "A beautiful new dress," I whispered to Hannah as I stood while she pinned up the hem. "But I feel like I'm getting all dressed for my funeral."

"Or mine," she mumbled.

The final, sad day arrived. I was leaving Lisec for America. Yossel waited in his wagon. My first stop would be in Stanislav to visit Mima Civia. Avram and Chaim cried and begged Mama to take them to Stanislav. But Mama didn't have the pfennigen it cost to take the boys in the wagon and back again. They were to stay with neighbors.

Tears streamed down their cheeks. "Take us with you. Please, Sarah."

"I can't." My tears matched theirs. "Mama has no money."

They clung to me. "We'll hide inside your coat."

I laughed through my tears, pried their fingers open, and released their hands. I bent to hug Avram and kiss Chaim as our neighbors tenderly held them.

"One day, I'll send for you."

"No, no! We'll never see you again!"

"Don't say that," I scolded. "Don't even think that."

Everyone in our village came to say good-bye. They called their best wishes. Were my brothers right? Would I never see Avram and Chaim again?

In the wagon, Mama sat with lips pressed together, her jaw stiff. Hannah and I sat close together. I looked at the houses of my village. I waved to the families and friends who had come to say good-bye. Would I ever again see these people who had known me since my birth?

It was almost dark when we arrived at Mima Civia's house and were greeted with smothering hugs. Mima Civia was taller than I, and I usually dreaded her greetings. I was always lost within her huge bosom, and I came out gasping for air. But today, I didn't mind.

"Why so sad?" She smiled. "Hannah is off to start a new life."

"No, Civia," Mama said. "There has been a change."

"How can there be a change? Hannah has Benjamin's tickets, doesn't she? Hannah has her passport, doesn't she?

The letter you wrote told me that."

"It would be better for me if Hannah stays. I couldn't manage without her. Sarah is going."

I began to cry again. Mima Civia put her arms about me. "So, you are a substitute, Sarah? Well, don't cry. There's a reason for everything." She held me close. "Meanwhile, you'll stay two nights, and we'll have a loving good-bye time."

We sat at the large dining room table and listened again and again to the reasons for my going to America. I felt as though Mama was putting a knife in my heart each time she repeated the story. Finally, Mima Civia announced, "That's enough. I've heard your reasons too many times, Leitcha. I'm going into the kitchen to cook all of Sarah's favorite food. If you want to help, that's fine."

The next two days were filled with food and Mima Civia's stories of her children and of Mama and Papa. Hannah was bored with these tales we had heard a hundred times. I listened carefully. I would carry these stories with me to America, and I didn't want to forget a word.

The last night in Stanislav, Mima Civia gave me her cameo. For as long as I could remember, she had worn that cameo on her dress. Now, she pinned it to *my* dress.

"This was my wedding cameo, Sarah, and I wish for you

the best of everything." She held me at arm's length. "When you are sad in your new life, my cameo will remind you of me. My memory will bring you good luck."

How would a cameo bring me good luck? Did she really believe that? I hugged her anyway. "Thank you, Mima Civia. A part of you will go with me to America."

The next morning we all walked to the train station. Mima Civia carried a basket filled with my favorite food. The trip would take four days and three nights from Stanislav to Hamburg. Mima Civia was determined that I reach the ship in good health and well fed.

Each step of the way, Mama gave instructions. "Be sure to write the minute you arrive in America. Don't talk to strange men. Don't lose your passport. Watch where you walk." Her warnings didn't stop until we reached the train and the conductor told me to get on board. But did she really care what happened to me?

I kissed Mama. She hugged me and whispered, "I really do love you, Sarah." Her wet cheek pressed against mine. "You have been a good daughter. Someday you will understand."

I kissed Mima Civia, then she and Mama wept together. Hannah and I hugged and sobbed. I promised to save my money and send for her, Mama, and the boys. I didn't want to let go of her. How could I, a twelve-year-old, leave my home, my family?

"All aboard!" The conductor took hold of both my elbows. He lifted me off the platform with Mima Civia's basket and my new cloth bag and set me in the train.

I slid the basket under the bench, clutched the cloth bag to my chest, and waved out the window. "Good-bye, Mama! Good-bye, Hannah! Good-bye, Mima Civia!"

The train started with a jolt. I leaned out the window and waved until the station was out of sight.

There were two long benches, one on either side of the train car, and I faced people who were facing me. I kneeled and looked out the window so no one could see what I was feeling. The train would take me to Hamburg where a ship was waiting to take me across the Atlantic Ocean to America. What if the ship sank in the middle of the ocean? Who would find me? Who would cry for me? Why did Mama send me away when Hannah wanted to go? Mama said someday I would understand, but I didn't understand now, and I would never understand. I leaned my head against the window and looked out. Fields of wheat flew past.

I had never seen life or land this far from home. We continued on through unending wheat fields. Peasants standing shoulder high in wheat stopped their work and waved. Children on wagons laughed, waved, and shouted as we passed. It didn't look much different from the people or the land I had left behind. I thought of Mama, Hannah, Avram, and Chaim. I thought of Papa. Did he know what was happening?

The woman sitting next to me put her hand across my back. "There, there," she said. "It's hard to leave home."

I turned to face her. She was younger than Mama. Her dark hair peeked out from under her flowered hat.

I nodded. How did she know what I was thinking?

"Where are you going?"

"America," I whispered.

"America?" Her eyes opened wide. "So young to go to America alone."

I put my hands over my face as if to erase the scene.

"There, there." She smiled. "My name is Frau Rivkin. We will be friends on the train." She took off her hat and placed it in a round hatbox.

I tried to return the smile.

At night, I slept where I sat, my head against the window. It was a fitful sleep of curves, bumps, and strange noises. When the sky lightened, I awoke. I was stiff, and my bones ached when I stood. I stretched tall and looked around. People were beginning to move.

Frau Rivkin looked up at me. "Did you sleep?"

"A little."

"It's difficult to sleep on a swaying train. Look! We're coming into the city."

I put my head out the window. Towers! There were cathedrals with towers sweeping the sky. I couldn't believe people could build such tall towers. And then a cross, sometimes two or three crosses, on top of the steeples. I tried to count them. Impossible. I had never known there were such huge buildings that seemed to touch the sky.

Was this what America would look like? Would I become lost in a jumble of tall buildings when I reached America?

The train pulled into the station where a large sign hung: KRAKOW.

Some people stood and walked to the doors. Some opened cloths filled with food and began to eat. A few had baskets like mine. There was a happy feeling—everyone eating, talking, laughing.

I took Mima Civia's basket from under the bench. There was enough food for three girls, not just one all-alone twelve-year-old. I bit into the bread.

Frau Rivkin opened a small basket. "Pretend it's a picnic," she said, smiling.

I laughed.

"Will someone meet you in America?"

"My uncle," I stammered.

"Well, you see, your uncle will take care of you."

How did she know Uncle Benjamin would care for me? He expected Hannah, who could work a sewing machine and care for herself. What if Uncle Benjamin didn't want me? My own mother didn't want me. Why would an uncle care?

"You will begin a new life, dear," Frau Rivkin said, smiling. "America is a land of milk and honey. They say the streets are paved with gold."

"How do you know?" I mumbled, my mouth full of bread.

"That's what they say." She motioned toward Mima Civia's basket. "Now, eat more than bread. It's still a long way to Hamburg."

I ate what I could and pushed the basket back under the bench. I stood and stretched. Thoughts of my last night at Mima Civia's flooded my mind. I touched her cameo. "Good luck," I whispered.

I looked around. New people were getting on. They looked no different from those in Lisec, except they wore nicer clothes. Would people in America look the same as these people?

I stretched again, my arms over my head. My passport

said I was Hannah and I was sixteen years old. Was my name going to be Hannah in America? Would I never be twelve-year-old Sarah again?

Suddenly, the train doors slammed shut. "All aboard!" came the call, answered by a blast of the train whistle. The jolt of the train's movement nearly threw me to the floor. I sat down on the bench.

"Next stop Breslau," said my neighbor.

"Breslau? I thought the next stop would be Hamburg."

"The next stop is Breslau," she said, smiling. "Then Berlin, then Hamburg."

I kneeled on the bench and looked out the window. Thoughts buzzed around in my head. "Breslau. Berlin. Hamburg. Hamburg, that's where the ship is waiting." My forehead on the glass, I whispered, "I don't want to go to America, and Mama doesn't want me at home. When the train stops at Hamburg, I won't get off—I'll return to Stanislav. Mima Civia loves me; she'd let me live with her."

We passed through green forests; a light summer rain splashed against the windows. The train moved on to open fields of grain. Here, too, peasants waved from their work, children stood in wagons, and girls shook their babushkas in the wind.

In the late afternoon, we approached Breslau, passed

flour mills and factories, and entered a city of beautiful buildings. Again, tall towers seemed to point toward heaven with their golden crosses. At the station, there was another exchange of passengers and another call, "All aboard!"

My second night on the train, I used my bag for a pillow. Again, there was no Mama to kiss me good-night. No Hannah, with whispered secrets. No little brothers. Sleep came as the train rolled on toward Berlin.

I woke with a start. The sun shone brightly through the windows. People were arranging their bundles. There was hurried movement and a feeling of excitement. I looked at Frau Rivkin.

"Where are we?"

"Berlin, my dear. Beautiful Berlin."

"We're in Germany?" Night had taken me across a border.

"Look, it's wondrous."

We were close to the center of the city. Again, there were church towers and tall buildings. Flowers were everywhere. "Oh, look!" I shook my neighbor's shoulder. She stood and looked to where I pointed. In the distance, it was as though a street was made of yellow flowers.

"Those are the lovely linden trees with their tender,

fragrant flowers. They were planted down the middle of the avenue, and they are very special."

I thought of Lisec with its dirt paths and very few flowers. I was in a different world.

The Berlin station was huge. There were more tracks and more trains than I could even imagine, and the noise was terrible.

By the time the "All aboard!" was shouted, we had walked on the station platform and washed in the restroom.

The train started with the jolt I now expected. It would be another day and another night until we reached Hamburg. The time seemed to fly. Frau Rivkin and I slept, leaning against each other.

"We're almost there," came whispered words. "We must travel through the city to the harbor."

I heard the words. I felt numb. "How do I get to the ship?"

"If you have a ticket," said Frau Rivkin, "there will be an important-looking man in an important-looking uniform who will take you from the train station to your ship."

I peered out the window. More steeples, more golden crosses, and more tall buildings that made the city of Hamburg.

My chest knotted in fear.

The train stopped. I stood. What was I to do next?

"I'll stay with you, my dear. We'll wait for the ticket master together," Frau Rivkin said as she carefully put her flowered hat in place.

Mima Civia's basket was still under the bench where I had sat, where I had slept. "Good-bye, Mima Civia," I whispered. I pushed the basket further under the bench with my foot. I wouldn't need a Ukrainian basket in America. I rubbed the cameo.

Frau Rivkin and I stood next to the train. A man dressed in a blue uniform came toward us.

"Here comes the ticket master. He'll put you on your ship," she said as she hugged me. "Good luck in America."

I watched her walk away, her flowers bouncing in a field of other hats.

The man in the uniform clicked his heels. "Welcome to Hamburg."

I almost laughed. He'd actually clicked his heels!

"May I see your passport and your ship's ticket?"

I reached into my bag and brought out the passport and ticket.

"Hannah Kamornick?" he read from the passport. He compared it to my ship ticket.

I nodded. What if he discovered I was not Hannah? What would happen to me?

"Small for sixteen years."

I swallowed hard. Would he let me on the ship with Hannah's passport?

"You'll have to grow up fast in America. Come along."

The man walked quickly, and I had to run to keep up with him. Then I saw the huge white ship. *Kaiserina Victoria Augusta* was painted in gold and black letters on the side. It looked like a fairy-tale castle that sat on the water. I couldn't believe this beautiful ship would take me, Sarah Kamornick, to America.

I followed the man up the gangplank to another man in a white uniform, who received the ticket and looked at my passport.

"Hannah Kamornick?"

I nodded.

"Sixteen years old?"

I nodded.

"Small for sixteen years."

I nodded again.

The white-uniformed man smiled. "If you eat all the ship's food, maybe you'll fatten up by the time we reach America." He motioned with his gloved hand. "Follow me."

We walked down dozens of narrow stairs and then through a long corridor. "Here is your cabin. You will share it with five young women. Do you read German?"

I nodded.

"Read the signs." He pointed to the walls in the walkway. "Toilets that way, wash basins next door to the toilets. Find the signs that lead you to the dining hall. You will all eat together." He closed the door.

The room was empty except for six beds, three stacked on top of one another against one wall and three stacked against the other wall. They looked as if they would fall over when the ship moved. There was a round window on the wall between the beds. It was shut tight. The room felt stuffy.

I sat on the closest bed and wondered if I was being punished for some awful sin I had committed. Was it a sin to pretend I was Hannah? Papa had said we must always be honest, and the most important part of honesty was to be one's self. Well, I was trying to be honest to myself, but I didn't know how I could be honest if I was using Hannah's passport. The ticket master thought my name was Hannah. That important man in the white uniform thought my name was Hannah. When I arrived in America, would I become Sarah again?

What name should I tell the girls I would share this room with? Sarah, my real name? Hannah, my passport name? I took a deep breath and made my decision. On board the *Kaiserina Victoria Augusta*, I would be Hannah. I must wait and see what name I would answer to in America.

Two girls came in, their cheeks wet with tears. It was strange, but I felt relieved that others shared my sadness.

The door opened again, and three more girls came in. A tall one with a black braid wrapped around her head said, "What are you all crying about? We're on the most beautiful ship in the world, and we're sailing to a shining new life."

"How do you know our life will be so good?" I demanded.

"Everything is good in America," she said.

One girl, with blue eyes and two long blond braids, sobbed, "But what will happen in America? I heard there are men who kidnap girls and take them for slavery."

Black Braid laughed. "You don't know that's true. We have to live for today, and we will be on this ship for fourteen days.

If you want to sit and worry, go ahead." She looked at each of us and grinned. "My name is Manya, and I'm the one girl in a family of six brothers. I lived on a farm north of Warsaw." She stood head and shoulders above me and seemed double my width.

I said my name was Hannah and that I came from Lisec, a village close to Stanislav.

"I'm going to my cousins who live in New York," Manya announced. "Who will meet you, Hannah?"

"My uncle and aunt."

Manya looked at the two tearful girls. They told us they were cousins from Lublin, north of Stanislav. They stood holding hands. I felt jealous, for they had each other.

"My name is Shoshana," said the blue-eyed girl, "but everyone calls me Shana. My oldest brother left for America a long time ago, and I'll live with him and his family." She turned to her cousin.

"I'm from the same village as Shana. When my parents heard she was going to her brother in America, they wrote to our cousins, who sent me a ticket." She looked at Shana. "If they don't like me, what will happen to me? If I don't like them, what can I do?" Her lip trembled.

"So, what's your name?" asked Manya.

"Annie."

Manya turned to the girls who had followed her into the room. They were both round as dumplings, and their smiles were comforting. They did not seem at all fearful—so different from me!

"I am Sophia," announced the first. She nodded toward her companion. "Marina and I are going to my older brother in New York. He sent for both of us."

Marina smiled. "Sophia's brother and I will be married."

"Married?" I was astonished. She looked no older than Hannah. "You are going to be married?"

"Oh, yes!" Marina laughed. "I'm sixteen years old, and I have known Alexandor for all of my life."

"Back home in Kiev, my house is next to Marina's house," said Sophia. "We went to the same primary school."

"Alexandor helped me with my lessons." Marina smiled.

"Lessons and . . . something else?" Manya grinned, and we all laughed together.

Marina's face turned red. Manya had embarrassed her; even so, I was envious. Marina knew where she was going and the man she would marry. I stood in silence.

"There are six bunks." Manya pointed. "Let's choose our beds. Then we'll go out for our last view of Europe."

I had already chosen mine. Annie and Shana took the

bunks above me, Manya chose the bunk across from me, and Sophia and Marina were above her.

We walked to the front of the ship where we could see the Hamburg harbor. It was the last we would see of this part of the world.

"We are beginning a new life," Manya sang out. She waved her arms in the air as though she were helping the ship to move.

As we left the shore, I felt the gentle movement of the River Elbe. A soft breeze touched my face. The wind seemed to be blowing away a life that would never return.

Out of the harbor, the ship continued to roll evenly. We watched green fields and small villages pass by until Helgoland Bay welcomed us to the North Sea and the Atlantic Ocean.

It seemed unnatural to sleep with five strangers in a small room with beds stacked atop each other. At home, there was only Hannah and me in a bigger bed, in a larger room. I folded my coat and dress and placed them with my bag under the pillow. I was afraid someone would take my new clothes and I would have only my underwear when I arrived in America.

I eased beneath the cover. I heard Shana and Annie crying. The ship rocked me to sleep.

A pounding jolted me awake. "Breakfast!" someone called outside the door. For a moment, I expected to be at home, my brothers jumping up and down in the hall outside my bedroom door. Happenings of the past days rushed back. I turned away from the wall and sat up.

We all stood up at the same time. The six of us giggled as we bumped into each other, trying to keep our balance. It was strange to try to dress in a tiny room with five other girls.

"There's no air in here," I said. "It smells." More giggles followed as I pulled the handle of the round window. The cold ocean air blew into the room.

"That's better," I said.

"Not like home," mumbled Shana.

"Not like home," Annie sniffled.

"If you continue your crying," Manya spoke in a harsh voice, "when we land in America, your eyes will be red and you'll look as if you are sick. Do you want to fail the medical inspection and be sent back alone?"

Annie stopped crying and bit her lips together.

We divided up; three of us sat on my bed, and three faced us on Manya's bunk. We put on our shoes and tried to lace them up. The rolling ship caused us to fall against each other and explode into laughter.

"Let's go," said our self-appointed leader. "Have you towels? No? Well, we'll use mine. One towel, six girls."

We had to wait in line at the washroom, our backs pressed against the wall. The ship was never still, and I struggled to keep from falling. Finally, one sink was empty. We burst out laughing again as we washed, trying to keep our balance.

In the dining hall were ten long tables that seated twelve people on each side. There were so many people, so much noise, so many voices! Huge bowls of porridge sat in the middle of the table. Manya grabbed one bowl, and we ladled what we wanted into waiting dishes. It tasted awful. I forced myself to swallow it. Shana and Annie paled, pressed hands to their mouths, and ran from the room.

Manya laughed. "No stomachs."

Suddenly, sourness rose into my mouth. I followed the other two outside. In misery, we hung over the ship's railing, sick to our stomachs. The strong wind blew wisps of our retching back in our faces.

Manya and Sophia rescued us. We stumbled into the washroom where Marina was waiting with the towel. Cold water felt good on my face.

"Are you all right?" asked Manya. "Do you need to lie down?"

Shana and Annie nodded.

"I'm better," I said, hanging onto the sink.

"Come. Fresh air will do you good." Manya put her arm around me, and we stumbled our way to the third deck, our hands against the walls.

I saw a family ahead of us, falling against each other, shrieking at their imbalance. The faces of Mama, Hannah, Avram, and Chaim flashed before me. And Papa. I wondered if he could see me on board this beautiful ship. Despite my roommates, I felt alone.

For the next two weeks, we walked like drunkards through the labyrinth of corridors, making up stories of what our lives would be like in America. Every story ended the same: a handsome man and marriage.

After days of walking the deck of the *Kaiserina Victoria Augusta*, we felt this huge white castle had become like the villages we had just left. We knew each corner of the

beautiful ship, nodded to the seamen on our deck, and smiled at passengers we saw every day.

We ran in procession around and around the ship's third deck, bumping into passengers, dodging mothers with their babies. My little brothers loved "touch and go," and as the six of us raced over the deck, I wondered if they, too, were chasing each other.

When we played "hide and seek," Marina found the smallest places we might hide. More often than not, our giggles led the seeker to find us. Then we raced to the ship's rail to run "home," safe.

The six of us would finally collapse on the deck and begin our hand clapping with a song Sophia's grandmother had taught her.

> *A golem lives in our house, our house, our house.*
> *A golem lives in our house all year long.*
> *He bumps and he jumps and he thumps and he stumps.*
> *He knocks and he rocks and he rattles at the locks.*
> *A golem lives in our house, our house, our house.*
> *A golem lives in our house all year long.*

Would there be a golem in my life—an unknown force I could or could not control?

The last night on shipboard, the six of us spoke quietly at the rail. Twinkling stars added to the excitement of our thoughts about what America would bring. Would America be frightening? Shana, Annie, and I were already frightened. Would America be a sad place for us? That was an unknown. Or would our arrival be filled with happiness? Marina and Sophia smiled. They knew.

It was difficult for Manya to remain still. "Remember your first tearful meeting?" She turned to me. "Look how your tears changed to laughter."

"Ooh," I moaned, "and that awful sick stomach."

Shana and Annie laughed. "Thank heavens that's gone."

We held onto the railing as we looked out into the ocean's darkness. After two weeks, our balance on this gently rolling ship still had not been perfected.

"To bed, to bed," sang Manya. "Tomorrow will be a day to remember. Our first steps on American soil!" We stumbled toward our cabin, too excited to sleep.

I stood next to my bunk and folded my dress. My fingers felt the collar to rub Mima Civia's cameo. "My cameo! My cameo is gone!"

I tore the blanket from the bed and searched the mattress. My friends shook the blanket, crawled on the floor, and felt under the beds. "It's gone," I whispered. "Tomorrow we arrive in America, and my good-luck cameo is gone."

"Get dressed," ordered Manya. "Follow me."

Single file, we made our way down the rocking corridor to the dining hall. Workers were cleaning in preparation for breakfast.

"Who is in charge?" asked Manya. A young man pointed to an older man.

I was pushed forward, and I told my tearful story.

"Nothing has been found," the man said, "and if your cameo is so beautiful, it may never be returned. But I will report your loss to my superior."

Manya put her arm about my shoulders. "Be brave. We'll pray that your cameo will be returned."

We walked slowly back to our room.

In bed, I prayed the kind man would find Mima Civia's cameo. When I landed in America, I would need all the good luck I could find.

As I lay waiting for sleep, I felt this journey was not real. One of the happiest times of my life had been the past two weeks with five strangers. We had become friends because we needed to be friends. Would we see each other in America? I wondered what friendship was like in America. Was it quickly made and then forgotten?

The breakfast call woke us. We rushed to dress and wash and hurried to the dining hall to look for the older man. We didn't see him. I went to the kitchen door to ask for him. No one knew where he was.

Manya squeezed my hand. "Try not to cry. Tears will spoil the good times we had together."

"America!" A shout rang out. We ran out of the dining hall, up the stairs to the railing. In the distance was the Statue of Liberty. Everyone was crying, laughing, and calling out, "America!" over and over again.

The ocean was no longer empty. There were ships of all sizes. Two tugboats came out and attached themselves to the *Kaiserina Victoria Augusta's* sides with ropes. The tugs began to guide us into the harbor.

Our hands in the air, we screamed as we jumped up and down. Then, suddenly, I saw what I had been looking for. I grabbed Manya's hand. "Look at that woman! She has my cameo pinned to her dress."

The woman stood with a boy about my age. "Come on!" Manya called to the other girls. We encircled the woman and her son. Manya, head and shoulders taller than both of them, stood in front of her.

"What do you want?" asked the woman fearfully.

"What do you want?" asked the boy, trying to be a man for his mother.

"Where did you get that cameo?" growled Manya.

"It's none of your business," the boy said.

"If that cameo's not yours, it is my business." Manya doubled her hands into fists.

"My son gave it to me." The woman looked at the boy. "He found it."

"Where did you find it?" Manya faced the boy, her voice softening a bit.

"Under the table where we eat," the boy said.

I sighed. "It must have come undone and fallen off my dress."

Manya spoke more calmly. "I'm sorry for getting so angry. That's my friend's good-luck cameo her cousin gave her. It's from Stanislav."

Manya looked at me, then at the woman again. "The cameo is my friend's memory of her family."

"Of course," said the woman. "We all need our memories." She took off the cameo, and Manya pinned it to my dress.

"There," Manya said. "Good luck is with you."

The Statue of Liberty stood beautifully tall as the two tugboats guided our ship past her and into the docks of New York Harbor. In our excitement, we pushed against the rail.

A loud voice called out in German, "Only first- and second-class passengers may depart here!"

The crowd around me called out in German, Polish, Russian, and Yiddish, "Why? Why?"

Manya grabbed my hand and looked at me. I shrugged my shoulders.

Again, the loud voice shouted. "Third-class passengers must go through Ellis Island!"

Now we all moaned. It would mean more time until we were allowed into America.

"What if they won't let us in?" were the whispered worries.

"Third class should not take long!" came the shouting

voice. "Just follow directions!"

Another rumbling of voices.

"You will leave the *Kaiserina Victoria Augusta* to take a smaller boat to Ellis Island!" the shouting voice instructed.

The six of us walked single-file down the gangplank of the beautiful ship to board a small boat. A man counted as he tapped each of us on the shoulder, then raised his hand. The remaining passengers stopped. Fifty people were all this boat could carry. We stood pressed together.

It was a short ride. We stepped from the boat to the landing at Ellis Island and entered a huge room. In my wildest imagination, I could never dream up such a great hall. To me, it appeared as big as the entire village of Lisec.

We were told not to walk away. We had to pass a health examination.

"Why do we need a health examination?" I asked my friends.

"Must be to see if we're healthy."

"Of course I'm healthy," I laughed. "And look at Manya. Don't tell me she's not healthy."

We moved forward slowly. At last, a woman dressed in white smiled at me. "I'm the nurse. Please come with me." I looked back at my friends and followed.

The nurse and I entered a room that was all white: white

walls and tiled floor, white cupboards with glass doors, and a long table. The room looked and smelled strange.

A man was waiting. The nurse said he was the doctor. She told me to unbutton my dress.

I felt shamed. Never, never had anyone but Mama or Hannah seen my body. Here was a strange man, looking at my naked body. My face felt hot, and I began to cry.

"I won't hurt you," said the doctor.

He listened to my chest, asked me to breathe, and tapped my back. The doctor in Lisec always wore a black suit, and he never listened to a person's chest unless that person was half-dead. I choked down my embarrassment.

The doctor continued to examine me. He looked in my eyes and then carefully pulled up my eyelids. He parted my hair and examined my scalp.

He smiled. "You are just fine, young lady. A little small for sixteen years, but you'll grow up quickly in America." He looked serious. "I'm sorry I frightened you, but we must be certain only healthy people enter the United States."

I buttoned my dress and quickly put on my coat.

"You can go now," the nurse said, pointing toward the door.

Once again, I was in that immense hall. A man in uniform took me to a desk. Another man looked at my passport. "Where are you going, Hannah?"

Hannah, that's me, I told myself. "To my uncle."

"Will he come to Ellis Island?"

I nodded and gave the man the letter and the picture Uncle Benjamin had sent to Mama.

"Good," said the man. "Here's an address where we can reach your uncle in case he doesn't come for you." He wrote the address on a piece of paper. He handed me Uncle Benjamin's picture and his letter. "Go through that door, Hannah."

The next room was crowded. Many of the people I had eaten with, had bumped into, and had played games around on the *Kaiserina Victoria Augusta* were waiting there. I looked for my shipboard friends. I fingered Mima Civia's cameo. She had said it would bring me good luck. It was my good luck that the cameo had been returned. Did luck happen only once in a lifetime?

I watched the door I had come through. "Manya!" I called when I saw her crown of black braids. We hugged as though we hadn't seen each other for years and years.

"There's Shana!" Manya waved, then shouted, "Shana!"

We waited, watching for our other shipboard friends.

"Where's Annie?" Shana was worried. "She was right behind me."

The three of us pushed our way back to the doctor's door. I knocked. The door opened. "Where's our friend Annie?" I asked. "We're worried about her."

"Come in," the nurse said.

Annie sat on the long table. She was crying, and she reached out for Shana.

"Your friend's eyes are very red," said the nurse. "We are concerned she may have a contagious disease called 'pinkeye.' She must remain in the hospital until we are certain she is not sick."

"Ooo," cried Annie, harder than she had cried before.

"Her eyes are so red because she's been crying for more than two weeks," I said. "She's not sick."

"Even so," the nurse went on, "she must stay here until her eyes are normal again."

"Can I come and visit her?" Shana asked.

"And who are you?"

"I'm Annie's cousin."

"Who will you be with in America?"

"My brother."

"You and your brother may visit Annie in the hospital."

"And when can she leave the hospital?"

"When her eyes are no longer pink."

Shana hugged her cousin. "No more crying, Annie."

Out in the huge hall again, I turned to Shana. "I don't know how Annie can stop crying. Just to be left there is enough to make anyone cry."

"Hannah!" I heard my name and looked into the crowd. "Manya!" Hands were waving in the air. "Shana!" The three of us recognized the shouters.

"Marina! Sophia!" We made our way over to the two of them.

"Where's Annie?"

"The doctor thinks she has pinkeye," I said. "She has to stay in the hospital until her eyes are better."

"When she stops crying, her eyes will get better," Shana said.

"Listen," said Manya. "We'll be leaving soon." She took out a piece of paper and a pencil from her bag. She tore the paper into pieces and wrote as she spoke. "I'm giving each of you my address. You do the same." Manya smiled. "That way, we can connect once we are settled."

We shared Manya's pencil, wrote our names and addresses on pieces of paper, and passed them around. It was as though a pact had been made. We would meet again.

A hush fell over the room filled with women, men, and once-noisy children. A woman in uniform stood on a platform with a handful of papers. "Listen for your name," she called out in German, Polish, and Russian. "When you hear your name, walk over to me. Someone has come for you."

She shouted names. Screams erupted after each name was recognized. I felt my heart race as I waited, then disappointment when the name called wasn't mine.

Sophia and Marina jumped in the air. "Here! Here!" They hugged the three of us, promised to write, and pushed their way toward the woman.

Where was my Uncle Benjamin?

Shana was next. Her blue eyes filled with tears, and she touched her cheek to mine. "Good luck, Hannah," she whispered, and was gone.

The room slowly emptied.

Manya looked at me. "Do you suppose we'll be here to the bitter end?"

My throat felt tight. I rubbed my damp hands on my coat. Where was my uncle?

"Manya—"

She jumped, not waiting for her last name. "Here I come!" she yelled in Polish. "Good luck, Hannah. I will see you soon, God willing."

I stood all alone. What would become of me? I looked at the picture of my uncle and aunt. Perhaps they had decided they didn't want me. Maybe I would be sent to prison. Wasn't it against the law to use someone else's passport? Would evil men really come and kidnap me for slavery? I rubbed Mima Civia's cameo.

It grew dark. Everyone had left with loving relatives. I sat on a bench and sobbed. The woman in uniform came and sat next to me. "Who will come for you?"

"My uncle."

"Don't cry—your uncle will come."

I rubbed Mima Civia's cameo harder.

A tall man with a black hat stood in the doorway. The woman in uniform walked toward him. "I'll take her now," he said. "She's my relative. Come, we'll get the last boat to New York."

"That's not my uncle!" I cried. I held out Uncle

Benjamin's picture.

"I'll take you to your uncle," the man said in German. "Come, hurry!"

"No!" I shouted at the woman in uniform. "He wants to kidnap me!"

"What proof of identity do you have?" asked the woman.

"What proof do I need? That's Bertha, my wife's niece."

"No! No!" I screamed and screamed.

The woman called a guard, and the man ran away.

"Don't worry," said the woman. "If your uncle doesn't come, we'll find him for you. But for now, you'll have to spend the night here."

I followed her to a room filled with cots. "You'll be safe here." She pointed toward a wall with closed doors. "The washroom is over there."

One twelve-year-old girl in an empty room. I sat on the edge of a cot. "Hear, O Israel. The Lord is our God. The Lord is One." I said that holy prayer over and over again.

It was dark when I awoke. There was a small light in the ceiling. I looked about the room. A clock on the wall told me it was eleven o'clock. I was still the only one in this big, empty place. I hugged my coat for protection and curled up around my bag. I missed the bed I had shared with

Hannah. I missed Mama. I missed Avram and Chaim. "Oh, Papa," I whispered. "Why did you have to die?" I squeezed Mima Civia's cameo and cried myself to sleep.

Again, I opened my eyes to darkness. The room seemed so large, and I felt so small. It was three o'clock. Again the tears rolled down my cheeks. Mama always said people cried when they felt sorry for themselves. Well, it was true. I felt sorry for myself, and I was crying. I slept again.

"Hannah Kamornick!"

I jumped up. The woman in uniform stood next to the cot. "Someone to take you home, Hannah."

I ran to the door. A man and a woman stood in front of me. I looked at the picture of my uncle and aunt. There they were, just like in the picture.

"Oh, Uncle," I whispered, and we hugged each other. Auntie joined in, and the three of us stood as one.

"We are here, Hannah," Uncle said. "There was confusion over the date of your arrival." He shook his head. "I'm so sorry." Uncle smiled at me. "Your aunt and I have come to take you home, Hannah."

We walked out into the sunlight. There stood the Statue of Liberty. She seemed more beautiful today. I had read about her in school. She held her lamp high and called to the homeless. Was I now at home?

I had held the secret of my name for so many days, days that now seemed a dream. I fingered Mima Civia's cameo. Should I tell my uncle and aunt that I was Sarah? What would they do?

"Uncle, I must tell you. I have been living a secret." I took a deep breath. "I am Sarah. Hannah is still in Lisec." I told him what had happened.

He put his hand on my shoulder. "Sarah, Hannah, they're only names. You are my sister's child. You will be my child. This is a new life, Sarah. You will change your way of thinking, you will change your way of living, you will change your way of being. But you were born Sarah, you have lived as Sarah, and you will be Sarah in America."

The boat took us from Ellis Island to New York Harbor.

"Look," I said to my aunt and uncle. "The Lady with the Lamp." I repeated the words of Emma Lazarus I had learned in school:

> *Give me your tired, your poor,*
> *Your huddled masses yearning to breathe free,*
> *The wretched refuse of your teeming shore.*
> *Send these, the homeless, tempest-tost to me.*
> *I lift my lamp beside the golden door!*

I, Sarah Kamornick, had arrived in America.
The year was 1910.